THE LOST WARDEN

EMERALD CITY DRAGONS [1.5]

WES GRANDMONT III

STUDIOS

The Lost Warden (Emerald City Dragons - Book 1.5) / Wes Grandmont III.

Published by Steamfire Studios

(an imprint of Wesley Grandmont III)

www.wesleygrandmont.com

This is a work of fiction. Any reference to historical events, real people or real places are used fictitiously. Other names, characters, places and events are products of the author's imagination and any resemblance to actual events or places or persons, living or dead, is entirely coincidental.

Cover Art © Copyright 2018 by Wesley Grandmont III.

First Print Edition 2019 v1.0.2

ISBN: 1-7320844-2-4

ISBN-13: 978-1-7320844-2-1

To my family and friends,
This story is for you.

INTRODUCTION

The events that unfold in *The Lost Warden : Emerald City Dragons - Book 1.5*, bridge the gap in time between the end of the story in *The Obsidian Ascent : Emerald City Dragons - Book 1* and the beginning of *Emerald City Dragons - Book 2*.

You will get more from this story and avoid some minor spoilers, if you have read *The Obsidian Ascent*, but it is not a requirement.

I've tried to provide enough information to help newcomers to the series still enjoy the adventure without re-treading too much ground for readers who are caught up on the previous books.

You can visit **wesleygrandmont.com/books** to grab a copy of *The Obsidian Ascent.*

Happy Reading!

Wes Grandmont III

INTO THE CALDRUN

ARÜN

B rody shoveled another pile of dirt onto Arün's body. "This is a horrible idea." His Scottish accent was thick with concern.

"It is." Arün agreed, but he needed to know what happened to his partner, Nadja—and this was the only way.

Arün lay in a shallow trench they'd dug in the soft soil of the remote Caldrun. Pacific Northwest pines rose around them into the late evening sky. It had taken the entire afternoon to hike the trail and another few hours of hunting before they'd located the toadstool ringed caldrun—a thin place separating this world and the world the Mages called Arburaan. The Mage Council kept these locations secret from the Wardens. But as the leader of the

Warden Guild, Brody had access to the restricted archives at the College. And Brody was just as worried about Nadja as he was.

The burly Scot tossed another shovelful of dirt onto Arün. "If the elves catch you, they'll kill you."

"Stop reminding me."

Brody's pursed lips disappeared behind his thick red beard. A deep crease formed between his brows.

Arün wished he could use a Thorngate for the trip, but the Mages had magical weaves in place around the gates to alert them if anyone tried to travel to Arburaan and the elves had wards on the other side to warn if any dracuns crossed over. But no one watched the caldruns—and for good reason —trying to cross via a caldrun, without specialized equipment, meant death. So it was the perfect way for Arün to slip across undetected.

The soil shimmered as Brody dropped another shovelful onto Arün. The weight of the dirt pressed against his legs. A normal human would die attempting an unprotected crossing, but the Mages had altered him. The blood of dragon offspring, known as dracuns, flowed in Arün's veins. It strengthened him, made him tougher and able to shift form. It meant he had a good chance of surviving what was about to come next.

"Put your mask on and make sure the oxygen is working." Brody motioned to the tank Arün clutched under his arm.

He gave Brody a wink. "Roger that."

Arün pulled the oxygen mask over his face. A thick hose connected it to the canister at his side. He turned the knob on the tank and sucked in a lungful of air.

"Don't be a hero, Arün. If she's in danger, get back here and we'll assemble a proper rescue party."

The mask muffled Arün's voice as he replied. "I won't do anything you wouldn't do."

"That's not reassuring," Brody said as he dropped a shovelful of dirt on Arün's chest.

"I'll be careful."

His friend added more soil. "I don't want to have to explain why you're missing. Get back here as soon as you can."

"I'll make it quick."

Brody nodded.

The Mages had discovered the caldruns more than a century ago. Before the Thorngates, they were the only way to reach Arburaan. The Mages called it "ground transportation"—they must have thought they were being clever. The crossing required burrowing through the caldrun. Energy from the pixie dust infused earth created a bridge to the other world. In the past, the Mages accomplished this with drilling machines that offered them protection during the crossing. Trying to access one of those machines would have raised too many alarms. So Arün had to do it the hard way—by being buried alive.

The Mages wouldn't approve this mission, but Nadja had been gone for six months. He and Brody were both worried. It was Arün's fault she was missing. He knew dracun had killed her family. And for years, Arün had hidden that he was half-dracun from Nadja—afraid of how she might react. He'd never been able to figure out a good way to explain to Nadja that part of him was related to the creatures she hated most in the world. And then it had been too late. She'd seen him shifted and the betrayal in her eyes had been unmistakable. Nadja had disappeared before he could explain.

He was almost buried now—only his face was still exposed. Brody lifted a final shovelful of dirt. "Godspeed, Arün."

The earth pressed in around his body, the dust tingled against his exposed skin. He smiled at his friend. "Whatever happens, Brody—thank you."

"Thank me when you get back." Brody dropped the dirt on Arün's head blocking out the sky.

Energy surrounded Arün—seeping into his pores. Everything was dark. Something beneath him gave way. The ground swallowed him as if he were sinking in mud. Soil flowed past his body. Tiny points of blue light winked by his mask, rising upward around him like luminescent water bubbles.

His body burned as if someone was rubbing it with sand paper. The dirt was abrading his skin as it flowed around him—tearing at his flesh. He had to shift or he would die. Arün focused, drawing into his mind. His head throbbed as the shift took hold. The pain subsided as he felt the cells in his skin change to hardened scales.

Half-dracun. Most of the Wardens were unaware of what Arün was, of the sacrifice he made to help the Mages understand how to make the Wardens more powerful. The newer Guild members never asked how the Mages figured out how to accelerate their healing and make them stronger and faster. They didn't know about the volunteers who had died or those, like him, that had survived and still lived with the consequences of the Mage's miscalculations.

It had been a sacrifice Arün had been proud to

make, even though it had made him an aberration—
a thing not quite human and not quite dracun. He
needed a chance to explain this to Nadja—for her to
understand that he wasn't one of the things she
hated most in the world. He was still her friend and
her partner.

The ground slipped around him. The dirt
churned blocking out sound, blocking out light.
Arün had to concentrate. If he shifted too far into
dracun form, he'd break the seal on the mask and
choke on dirt.

How much longer?

Something tugged at his leg. It moaned. The
sound sent a chill through Arün's body. It was one of
the things that lived in the place between the two
worlds. When he'd traveled through the Thorngates,
he'd heard them on the other side of the tunnel
walls. They sensed those crossing through their
realm. The tangled vine tunnels of the gateways
offered protection from them. The caldrun—offered
nothing.

Arün gritted his fanged teeth. He'd be dead in
human form. The moaning was getting louder. The
tugging on his leg was getting stronger, slowing his
descent into the ground. They were trying to stop

him from crossing. Arün's eyes went wide within the mask.

He shook his leg, but the soil pressed around him, restricting his movement. The wails intensified. Things grabbed at his body. Something tugged on the mask.

No.

Arün sucked in a deep breath of air and squeezed his eyes closed, just before the mask was ripped from his face. He fought the urge to yell. Soil flowed around him, but it was slowing. His chest burned from lack of air.

Then he felt wind against his back. Arün pushed against the dirt above him. His senses flipped as up became down and he rose out of the ground. Clawed hands with bleach-white skin tore at his clothes. He pulled his limbs out of the soil and rolled away gulping in a lungful of air. The emerald scales on his half-shifted body glittered in the rays of Arburaan's sunset.

He drew his Warden blade. His scryth. The runes on its surface glowed a brilliant blue. The scryth glowed green when dracun were close. Blue was a new color. Arün slashed at the groping arms that sprouted from the caldrun. They recoiled under the sparkling dirt. The runes on the scryth dimmed as the soil went still.

Arün stood and sheathed his blade. Enormous trees, the size of skyscrapers, rose around him. The chatter of insects and distant calls of strange animals echoed in the air. He'd survived the crossing, but now the real challenge began. This world was full of dangerous things. He brushed dirt from his clothes and withdrew the milkstone locket that Bezo had given him. Nadja had one just like it. The elven stone inside acted as a compass, guiding the bearers back to one another.

Arün opened the locket and angled it to catch the light from the setting sun. The swirling milky surface coalesced to form three dark spots along the edge of the stone. Each dot pointed the way to a different linked milkstone. The smaller ones pointed to Alley and Elek back on Earth. The darkest spot pointed into the forest—to Nadja.

Arün snapped the locket shut and then focused his mind, forcing his body to shift all the way back into human form. It was always strange to watch the green scales submerge beneath the surface of his human skin.

With luck he'd avoid the elvish wards designed to go off near anything with dracun blood. With luck he'd avoid the deadly creatures roaming the forest. With luck he'd find Nadja and repair their relationship. And with whatever luck remained, he'd bring her home.

Arün drew his gun and headed into the shadows between the trees.

And if his luck ran out, he had enough ammunition to share his misfortune with whatever crossed his path.

2

DARKWOOD CROSSING

ARÜN

Arün followed a worn trail that wove its way through the massive trunks of the towering trees. This part of the forest was called the Lower Darkwood. It was named for its location below the great cliffs of the Upper Plateau and for the deep shadows cast by the enormous interlocking bows of the trees. He stopped under a gigantic root that arched over the trail and pulled out the locket. The milkstone pointed southeast, toward the Elvish Capital.

Why did you go there, Nadja?

Her choice increased the difficulty of the mission. After the Ash War, the elves had sworn to kill any dracun on sight. It didn't matter that the dracun part of Arün was genetically engineered.

He'd have to work his way towards the Capital and avoid alerting the elves. Part of him wanted to quit. Was his relationship with Nadja worth risking his life? Arün wished he didn't have such a strong need for Nadja to know he hadn't betrayed her—that he wasn't a monster. Maybe it was because he hadn't been able to save his fiancée. Lyla had killed herself when she found out what he'd become. More than fifty years later, it was still painful. He couldn't lose Nadja too. He needed her to accept him—to know that he was still the same partner and friend that he'd always been.

The creatures in the forest went silent.

Arün looked around trying to make out movement in the surrounding undergrowth. The Mages cautioned against cutting through the forests of Arburaan and advised staying on the Scale Road, the network of dragon-scale paved highways that crisscrossed the realm. Cutting through the woodlands risked angering the pixies and encountering one of the dangerous species indigenous to the forest. Even with those risks, the Scale Roads where more dangerous for him now. The elves had reportedly setup wards along the roadways after their last visit. If he traveled the Scale Road, the elves would detect him long before he reached the Capital.

The only choice left was cutting through the woods. The only problem—the creatures that lived in the forest had created this trail. It was just a matter of time before one crossed the path.

A branch snapped in the underbrush.

It was close.

Arün dropped to his knee and raised his gun. He wished he was less exposed. At least the giant root arching over him provided protection.

Up ahead, the leaves of a droopy-leafed bush parted and a large spidery leg emerged. The exoskeleton was pale yellow. As the creature stepped onto the trail, Arün saw it had six legs attached to a long tubular body covered in bristly yellow quills. Stalks with eyes that looked human sprouted from the top of the creature's body.

Arün remained crouched and held his breath. He slipped the safety off on his weapon. If it attacked, he didn't know where to aim to kill it. He should have done more research.

The creature pushed itself up on its front legs to reach the droopy bush. A vertical slit on the smooth underside of its body tore off some leaves and chewed them.

A plant eater.

Arün exhaled. He lowered his gun. It was a herbivore, but the quills could do some damage if the creature was threatened. He'd need to wait a moment for the animal to leave before he could press forward.

It moved slowly as it consumed the leaves. Arün half-smiled. It was ugly, but cute. The quills reminded him of a porcupine.

I'm going to call you, Porky. It was ridiculous, but it made the thing seem less dangerous.

Suddenly, Porky's eyestalks swiveled towards Arün. They looked terrified. But, they weren't looking at him—they were looking past him.

Arün glanced over his shoulder.

A dark shadow filled the trail.

The towering predator's body was as big as a garbage truck and was held aloft by legs that were as long as telephone poles. It stalked forward. How could something so large, be so silent? The legs ended in sharp points that made no sound as they pierced the underbrush. A sinuous neck held its eyeless head low to the ground. It looked like a giant giraffe and a crab had decided to have a baby. The result was this long-legged monstrosity.

Arün raised his gun. His heart thundered in his chest. Would bullets have any effect? A hard carapace covered half the thing's body. Running seemed like it would not end well.

Porky squealed at the approaching creature and launched itself into the air.

The monster leaped over the root above Arün's head and skewered Porky as he tried to run up the trunk of one of the enormous trees. Porky's quills shot out of his body like arrows and bounced harmlessly off the monster's shell. The smaller creature's yellow limbs thrashed against the bark, not yet realizing it was already dead.

The monster stabbed at Porky again—tearing its body in two.

Arün ran.

He didn't know how long the kill would distract the monster, but he didn't want to be around when it finished with its current meal. Arün had to get through the forest. There were too many predators. Getting eaten was starting to seem less appealing than being executed by the elves.

He'd be safer if he shifted into dracun form, but there were two problems with that—the first was that the pixies might notice a dracun roaming their lands and alert the elves. The second was that he'd selected his clothes to help him survive the caldrun crossing, not to make it easy to shift. The fabric was designed to withstand ripping and abrasion. It was nothing like the clothing worn by the dracuns that worked with the Warden Guild. Their human garments were designed to unsnap along special seams as they transformed, removing the need for them to undress ahead of time to prevent destroying their clothes. Without the special seams, Arün's clothes would tear to shreds if he transformed in an emergency. If that happened, he'd need to stay in dracun form or spend the rest of the mission running naked around Arburaan.

He glanced over his shoulder. The monster was out of sight now.

Arün slowed his pace to a fast walk. Running was risky—it might attract other predators, and it made it impossible to scan the trail for any wards that the elves may have placed along the path. But he couldn't move too slowly either. The sun was sinking —and the most dangerous creatures hunted at night. Arün wished he'd been able to arrive earlier in the day.

Movement interrupted his thoughts—something deep in the woods on the right side of the trail.

The hair on his arms stood on end.

Arün crouched and waited.

Something black as night leaped between two of

the enormous trees. It looked like a shadow hugging one of the huge branches except for its four red eyes.

Arün swallowed.

A grek.

Brody had warned him about these creatures. Silent four-armed hunters that stalked their prey from the canopy. As big as a grizzly bear, but much faster. It had huge jaws lined with several rows of razor-sharp teeth and a chameleon-like tongue capable of grabbing animals from nearby tree limbs. They lived in the deep forest—this one must be hungry if it had been willing to venture so close to the edge of the elvish lands.

The grek stared straight at him.

At least he'd noticed it before it had gotten close.

Showing weakness would only make it more aggressive. Arün bared his teeth and crept down the trail while keeping an eye on the thing.

The grek jumped to a closer tree.

Arün forced himself not to break into a sprint. It was trying to get into a position where it could attack before he'd have time to react.

The sound of rushing water drew his attention for a moment. Somewhere up ahead was a fast-moving river.

Good.

Grek couldn't swim. If he could get across, the creature might abandon its pursuit.

Arün glanced back up to where the dark form had been clinging.

It was gone.

He searched the trees above him.

Stupid.

He'd taken his eyes of it for only a second. It could be anywhere now.

Get to the water.

Arün drew his scryth. With his blade in one hand and the gun in the other, he moved faster down the trail, scanning the canopy for movement.

The roar of water increased and then the path opened onto a wide flat ledge. A hundred feet below, a river churned through a deep gorge that cut through the middle of the forest. The root of one of the massive trees had grown over the chasm forming a natural bridge—the only visible way across.

Seated at the top of the bridge was a hulking form covered in inky black fur.

The grek.

It stood on its hind legs, spread its four arms wide and roared, then slammed its fists down on the root's mossy bark.

Arün nodded at the creature as he raised his gun. His heart was pounding. "Hey, fella."

The grek was only thirty feet away. It could close that distance in one jump. Brody's final warning about these creatures had been that they were fast healers. The only way to be certain they were dead was to cut off their heads.

Its lips peeled back revealing gleaming teeth. It was grinning at him. It probably expected him to run.

Arün took a step towards it.

Then another.

Mist from the churning water curled upward into the air between them.

The creature cocked its head.

Good. He'd surprised it.

Arün stepped forward again.

The grek stepped back. It was no longer sure of itself. Creatures in this forest only advanced on prey.

Arün stepped up onto the root bridge. He angled his blade so the light from the setting sun glinted off the elvish metal. The grek's gaze darted towards the weapon. The skin around its eyes wrinkled. Its reaction was more than an acknowledgment that Arün held something sharp—it was recognition. The grek had seen a scryth before.

Its posture changed. Now it looked ready to attack.

Great. Arün guessed that the last time the grek had seen one of these blades it must have eaten the owner.

He forced himself to relax.

The creature grinned at him again—then its orange tongue shot out of its mouth.

Arün only had time to raise his gun arm across his face. The tongue struck his forearm instead of his head. The sticky flesh clung to his coat sleeve and yanked him toward the creature's jaws.

Arün dug his heels into the bark of the bridge. The rapids churned below. The ugly orange tongue was reeling him in like a hooked fish and he couldn't reach across his body to slice at it without losing his footing. He had seconds to make a plan before the grek was close enough to bite off his arm.

The tongue dragged him another few feet forward.

Arün had an idea. If it failed, he would have to shift, but it was a risk worth taking.

He ran towards the grek. The creature's sticky tongue still stuck to his arm. At the last second he jumped off the bridge—out into the open air of the gorge.

The grek's eyes went wide. It dug its claws into the bark as the full weight of Arün's body yanked downward on its tongue.

Arün's momentum carried him forward. He swung below the bridge. The grek struggled to keep from getting pulled off the massive root as Arün's weight stretched out its tongue. As he arced upward, Arün twisted his body and slashed at the sticky orange flesh attached to his arm. Yellow blood sprayed through the air as the severed tongue retracted back into the creatures mouth.

Arün landed on the far side of the bridge just beyond the grek. It roared and charged at him. Yellow blood flowed between its teeth, but its tongue was already healing.

Arün fired his Drak-9 at the creature. The mini-railgun spat high velocity rounds into the grek's hide. It shrieked and recoiled trying to shield its body from the attack. Arün moved forward as he fired at the creature. It was healing almost as fast as he was wounding it.

It roared again and grinned.

Arün needed to end this. The grek would just keep coming unless he killed or frightened it.

Anger sent adrenaline flowing through his veins. He allowed his body to start the shift—felt the emerald scales pushing through his flesh—felt the pain of his skull expanding and his neck extending. His teeth lengthened into sharp fangs. The fabric of his clothes tightened against his body. Arün stopped the transformation.

The grek backed up, its eyes grew wide.

It knew what he was becoming.

Arün planted his feet and roared.

The grek leaped into the trees and disappeared into the distant shadows.

Arün reloaded and holstered the gun and then shifted back to human. Back to himself. He used his scryth to scrape the remains of the grek's tongue from the sleeve of his coat, then wiped the blade off on a patch of moss. He sheathed the weapon and finished crossing the bridge.

Elves had cleared the underbrush on this side of the gorge. The trail wound around the giant tree trunks with only scattered boulders breaking up the floor of dead leaves and ferns. They probably kept it clear to discourage creatures from roaming too close to the edge of the forest. It meant he was nearing the outskirts of the Capital. The farms and villages surrounding the city supplied food and a defensive buffer between the population center and the wilderness.

Arün quickened his pace. The sunlight was fading. He wanted to be clear of the woods before nightfall.

Minutes stretched by as he jogged through the forest. Ahead he could see a break in the trees and glimpsed an open field. He'd reached the edged. Just a few more moments and he'd be free of the Darkwood.

Arün sensed the change in the air a second before he felt it. It vibrated in a way that made his throat constrict.

A ward.

He froze and scanned the trees.

There—hanging from a limb high overhead. It looked like a wind chime, but the magical weaves etched into the metal tubes would signal the presence of a dracun or any other creature that represented a danger to the elves. He could try to avoid this one, but they were probably hung along the entire edge of the forest. He'd have to destroy one of them to move forward.

Disabling a ward was easy if it wasn't one designed to be used against you. It was much harder if you couldn't get close without setting it off. There was also the possibility that they'd been setup to cascade. Cascading would cause a ripple effect where each ward would trigger the others nearby. A cascade would raise an alarm across the entire countryside.

The vibrations in the air meant he was close to triggering this one. Arün backed up a few paces and drew his gun. Destroying the ward would likely set off a maintenance alarm, but anything could cause those—wind, downed tree limbs, animals. Arün aimed at where the chimes were tied to the tree and squeezed the trigger. The branch exploded in a shower of wood splinters and the ward dropped to the ground with a clatter.

Arün stepped forward, concentrating on the feel of the air.

Nothing.

He took another step.

Still nothing.

Arün continued edging forward expecting at any moment to sense tightness on his throat. It didn't come.

He'd gotten lucky, but for how long?

Arün holstered the gun and continued on the trail, keeping an eye on the overhead branches. The path ended between two of the massive trees. Beyond, a rolling field filled with iridescent corn-like plants stretched towards a distant elvish town.

Above the distant tree line, the towers of the Capital rose, dark against the waning orange glow of the sun. The twin moons were rising overhead, bathing the land in twilight.

Arün pulled out the milkstone locket and snapped it open. The dark spot that represented Nadja still pointed toward the Capital. It was going to be a challenge to get into the city undetected. He closed the locket and looked up.

An elven hunter stepped out of the cornfield, aiming an arrow at Arün's chest.

OUTSKIRTS

T he hunter cocked his head to the side. "Dus Warden?"

He wore a vest over a loose-fitting tunic. His white hair was pulled back into a short ponytail that exposed his long-tufted ears. Brilliant blue eyes squinted at Arün from beneath white brows. The hunter wasn't a member of the High Guard. His clothes lacked the refinement of the warriors that protected the Capital.

Arün pulled his coat aside and slid his scryth out of its sheath so the hunter could see the blade's runes. It proved he was a Warden and since it wasn't glowing, communicated that there was no nearby dracun.

The elf nodded at the blade. "Where come you from?"

The hunter lacked the mastery of English enforced by the High Court, but his choice to speak in Arün's native language was a sign of respect.

Arün raised a fist to his chest and bowed—an elven gesture of greeting. "I'm on a diplomatic mission." He lied.

The elf kept the bow aimed at Arün's chest and glanced at a crystal-studded bracelet strapped to his wrist. One crystal was glowing. "You break ward?"

Arün stared at the metal band and cursed his luck. The crystal had alerted the elf the instant he'd destroyed the chimes. What excuse would be good enough?

Arün nodded towards the forest. "A grek was following me. It knocked down the ward."

The elf glanced into the darkness between the trees. "Kill it?"

Arün showed him the sleeve of his coat where chunks of tongue still clung to the leather. "It almost got me. I injured it."

The elf nodded and lowered his bow. "It heal. Soon back. We go."

Great. The elf wanted to escort him to safety. The High Guard would be alerted and would detect his dracun genetics with one of their more sensitive blades. If he could knock out the elf and tie him up, Arün would have enough time to complete the mission. He needed to find the right moment before they reached the distant village.

Arün spotted a stone near his foot that was small enough to conceal, but large enough to bludgeon the hunter. He smiled at the elf. "I need to tighten my laces before we go."

He shifted his stance so that the stone was between his feet and then bent down and pulled on the laces of his left boot. As he moved his hands to the right boot, he palmed the stone off the ground.

The elf made a choking sound and Arün froze. He hadn't been subtle enough. The hunter had seen him grab the stone.

Arün looked up, expecting to see the elf's angry expression. Instead, an orange hunk of meat covered the hunter's face.

A grek tongue.

The beast clung to the trunk of a tree behind Arün. Its tongue would have struck his head if he hadn't bent down to tie his boot.

The elf clawed at the sticky orange flesh, trying to peel it off so he could breathe. Arün drew his scryth to chop at it, but before he could swing, the grek retracted its tongue, yanking the hunter up into the boughs.

Arün dropped the stone and drew his gun. It was too late. He heard a crunch as the creature bit down on the elf's head and the hunter's body went limp. The grek used two of its four arms to hug the elf's body against its dark hairy belly and then disappeared into the forest.

Arün holstered his gun and sheathed the blade. He'd never catch the creature, and the hunter was already dead. Arün felt a pang of guilt for destroying the ward that allowed the beast to approach undetected. He felt more guilty for feeling grateful for the creature's help.

Arün pressed two fingers to his lips, touched them to his chest and then held them to the sky. He didn't know the hunter, but he knew enough about elvish customs to know they reserved this gesture for honoring the dead on the battlefield. He turned away from the forest and waded into the field of glowing grain.

The blue glow of the crop coupled with the light of the twin moons overhead, bathed the field in a ghostly twilight. As the village grew closer, the sound of laughter drifted through the air. The elves were celebrating one of their countless holidays.

Arün didn't know what season they were in, but it didn't matter. The festivities might offer enough distraction to allow him to slip past the town with no one noticing.

As he emerged from the field, a line of laundry hung between two posts outside the closest cottage. Laughter came from inside, but the grassy yard looked deserted. Keeping low, he crossed the lawn and grabbed a cloak drying on the line. It was still damp but would conceal his human clothes. The fabric was purple and embroidered with a pattern of ivy and wildflowers.

Arün grimaced.

Elvish women wore this style during the High Holidays. A hunting cloak would have been better. He pulled the cape around his shoulders and fastened the carved wooden toggles at the throat to hold it in place. The wet cloth smelled of something that reminded him of lavender and pine. Arün raised the hood. It did a good job concealing his head at the expense of cutting off his peripheral vision.

Arün walked back towards the edge of the field. He had to stay out of sight and not look like he was sneaking around town—just an elvish girl out for a moonlit walk. Arün smiled to himself. He needed to find the stables and commandeer a horse—it would allow him to reach the Capital faster and reduce the chance of an elf identifying him.

Arün recalled what he knew about elvish towns. The villages were planned in a hub and spoke fashion—rings of buildings with streets between and main roads leading to the grassy commons at the center of the town. They built the outer buildings from heavy timber with thick shuttered windows and huge gates that could be closed to defend the village. The dwellings close to the commons would be more ornate, with flowing architecture that made them look more grown than built. The stables would be located on the outer ring.

Arün walked along the line of glowing grain, stopping every few paces to listen and scan for sentries. He smelled the stables before he saw them. The musky scent of the animals drifted through the night air. The Mages called the elvish steads *horses*, but they differed from the ones on Earth. Their hooves were split into three parts, they were covered in longer hair and they had an extra set of nostrils. Even though they looked different, they behaved and smelled the same.

Light and laughter spilled from an open window at the closest end of the stable. Arün peaked over the edge. Two elves sat on bails of hay. They were drinking from tankards and telling jokes he only half understood. Dozens of horses filled the stalls. Arün ducked under the window and walked toward the other end of the building. The stable was long enough that the elves might not notice if he entered from the other side.

A moment later he stood at the far entrance. It was dark. Twenty horse stalls spanned the distance to where the elves sat celebrating. A few piles of hay helped obscure the view down the wide aisle that ran the length of the stable.

The horse in the closest stall snorted at Arün.

"Easy, boy," he whispered. The creature could smell the bits of grek tongue still clinging to his jacket.

Arün lifted the stall's latch and dragged the gate open enough so that he could slip inside. The creature shied away as he entered. A bridal and saddle hung on the wall. They were similar in design to riding equipment on Earth, but with some slight differences. Arün whispered to the horse as he fit the bridal over the creature's head. He placed the saddle on the horse's back, adjusted the straps and then tightened the cinch.

The horse bucked.

Arün fell backward and tripped over a pale of water. The metal bucket clattered as its contents spilled onto the hay covered floor.

The laughter at the other end of the stable ceased.

Arün cursed as he peeked over the edge of the stall.

The elves were approaching. If they sounded the alarm—he shook his head. He couldn't let that happen. His Elvish wasn't good enough to talk his way out of the situation and he needed to avoid killing them.

Arün clenched his fists and crouched near the gate.

They were only a few stalls away.

"Tis brohan!"

One of them had noticed that the gate was unlatched.

Arün tensed.

The elf placed a hand on the top of the gate.

Arün launched himself against the door with every ounce of strength in his enhanced muscles. The gate crashed outward sending the elf flying into the stall doors on the opposite side of the aisle. Arün's cloak whirled around him as he jammed his boot into the second elf's inner-thigh. As the stablehand fell to his knee, Arün hit him with an uppercut. The elf collapsed on the floor in an unconscious heap. The first elf groaned and struggled to stand. Arün grabbed him from behind in a chokehold and held the elf until he went limp.

He lowered the stablehand to the floor and checked his pulse.

Still alive. Good.

Coils of rope hung from hooks on a nearby wall. Arün used them to bind each elf and then jammed rags into their mouths.

He whispered to them. "Mo'wen." *I'm sorry.*

The two stablehands didn't deserve the beating, but he didn't deserve to be killed just because a few extra chromosomes marked him as part dracun. He was lucky they had been drinking. Under normal conditions, elves were as fast as Warden and skilled in combat.

Arün rubbed the skittish horse on the nose and led it out of the stall. He'd need to get out of the town before someone discovered the unconscious elves. He mounted the horse and adjusted the cloak to hide his face and clothing, then nudged the beast into motion.

They exited the stable and headed out onto a road that formed one of the spokes leading to the center of town. Before they reached the center, Arün guided the horse down one of the side streets. This route would allow him to avoid the celebration as he skirted around the village. The curved street was quiet and lined with small cottages. Most of the windows were dark—the residents were probably attending the festivities.

Arün urged the horse forward. The faster he got out of the town—the better. He couldn't afford any more encounters with the locals. The horse accelerated to a brisk trot.

Arün felt the air vibrate and his throat constricted.

There was a ward nearby, but the horse was moving too fast to stop in time.

A crystal mounted on the door jamb of the nearest cottage flared brilliant white. The stone emitted a high-pitched tone that rose and fell. It caused the crystal on the door of the neighboring home to flare and then emit the same ear-splitting alarm.

The wards were cascading—Arün had less than a minute before every alarm around the town was triggered.

4

___

DISCOVERY

ARÜN

Arün snapped the reins and kicked his heels into the horse's sides. The animal sped to a gallop. Its hoofbeats thundered in the confines of the narrow street, mixing with the rise and fall of the alarms. As he passed each house the crystal on it flared and wailed.

The sound made him cringe. Each ward accused him of being something he wasn't. Could he convince Nadja of the truth? Would she listen, or raise the alarm too?

Elves tumbled out of the cottages with arrows knocked on bowstrings, but no one fired at him. The disguise was working. The flowery cloak marked him as an elvish maiden—who they assumed was being chased by something.

Good.

Arün estimated he was halfway around the town. He needed to get to the main road before the elves closed the gate. As long as they weren't shooting at him, he might make it.

As if in reply to his thought—an arrow flew past his head. Arün glanced over his shoulder. An archer chased him on horseback.

"Dus Dragun! Dus Dragun!" shouted the archer as she fired another arrow. It thudded into the leather padding of Arün's saddle. A few inches higher and it would have hit him in the lower back. If he kept giving the archer a clear line of fire, it was just a matter of time before one of her arrows hit its mark.

Arün rolled his eyes. The Ash War was how long ago? A hundred years at least. The elves behaved as if the dragons would attack at any moment—even though the Clans had all been exiled to Earth.

He approached an intersection and pulled the reins to the right, driving towards the celebration at the center of the town. The archer might be more reluctant to shoot, if a miss might hit one of her friends.

A massive bonfire lit the grassy commons. The perimeter of the crowded space was decorated with dozens of life-size figures woven out of thick wicker. Elves were dancing, singing and drinking. Loud music, song and laughter filled the air—it drowned out the noise of the wards.

"Dus Dragun! Dus Dragun!"

The archer wouldn't stop yelling. Arün wanted to shout back that she was mistaken and explain the difference between being born as a dracun versus having the genes of a dracun spliced into your own. It was the exact conversation he would have with Nadja, except the elf wouldn't understand any of it. Partly, because of his poor Elvish fluency, but mostly because genetic manipulation wasn't something the elves understood—their technology was purely based on weaves. They'd never had an industrial revolution. Their innovations centered on magic, not science. It was why they'd needed the Mages to help end the war with the dragons.

Arün snapped the reins of the horse and urged it to go faster. He pounded into the commons knocking drunken elves aside like bowling pins. The celebration erupted into chaos as the horse dodged around tables laden with food.

Arün felt bad for ruining the party, but as he'd hoped, the archer wasn't willing to fire. That would change in a moment. The darkness of the main road lay ahead. It offered both escape and a clear shot at his back. He needed something to protect his flank.

As he neared the road, the horse veered to avoid one of the wicker statues. Arün reached out and grabbed it. Picking up the heavy figure would have been an impossible feat without his enhanced strength, but with it, he easily swung the statue behind his back as he charged onto the road.

An arrow embedded itself in a nearby wall as he rounded the corner. He felt another hit the wicker figure. His heart raced.

The wards across the entire village were triggered now. Their squeal filled the air. He didn't want to kill any elves, but if he was forced to make a choice, the Drak-9 in his holster had a full magazine and he was an excellent marksman. He felt another arrow strike the statue. It still amazed him that even after they'd seen the effectiveness of human firearms during the Ash War, the elves still preferred bows and arrows.

The main gate leading out of the village was just ahead. Sentries flanked either side. They stepped into the road and lowered vicious looking spears.

Arün sighed and drew his gun.

He aimed at the thigh of the elf on the right and squeezed the trigger. The Drak-9 whirred, coughed and flashed bright green as it spat out a magnetically accelerated slug. A crimson hole blossomed on the sentry's leg. The elf dropped the spear and clutched at the wound. Arün aimed at the other elf. The second sentry dived out of the way.

He thundered through the gate. Something bright lit up the twilight as it arced past and embedded into the dirt on the side of the road.

A flaming arrow.

The mounted archer had been joined by two companions. Now clear of the town, they had apparently decided it was safe to play with fire.

More arrows followed. They thumped into the wicker statue, setting it ablaze. If Arün shifted form, his dracun scales could withstand the heat, but in a few minutes he'd need to drop the statue to keep from burning the horse. When that happened, the elves would fill his back with arrows.

Ahead, the spires of the Capital rose into the moonlit sky. They were more grown, than built. The elves had used magic to form the stones and had cultivated ivy, trees and other plants to grow along the surfaces. The city rested on the tip of a peninsula with tall cliffs that fell into the ocean. Ahead, the road curved through a grove of oak trees before crossing over a gorge that the Alga River had carved into the peninsula as it flowed out of the Darkwood and crashed into the ocean.

Arün's back felt hot. Sputtering flames from the burning statue cast long shadows on the road. The horse pounded onto the wooden bridge that crossed the river. Its hoofbeats echoed off the walls of the gorge.

A calvary approached from the other end of the span—the elven High Guard. Their captain, El'Iswald, had tried to kill Arün the last time he'd visited. Arün wasn't going to give him another chance. He banked the horse toward the bridge railing. The waters of the Alga frothed far below.

Arün tossed the statue aside and leaped off the horse. It was a dangerous move, but less dangerous than staying on the bridge with a bunch of murderous elves. He sailed over the edge and plummeted toward the river. The fall didn't take long. He plunged into the seething rapids. Frigid water soaked into his clothes. His body bounced off underwater boulders worn smooth by the river. Arün pushed himself upward. His head emerged from the water and he gasped for air.

The river picked up speed.

The falls! He would be carried over the edge if he didn't get out.

Arün kicked hard and swam towards the wall of the gorge. His water-logged clothes made it difficult to stay afloat. He fumbled with the clasp on the hooded cape. The rapids pulled at the heavy fabric. The toggle released, and the cloak swirled away.

Arün reached his hand toward a branch lodged between two nearby rocks—and missed.

The water turned to raging foam—and then he was falling.

He forced his body to partially shift into dracun form. If there were rocks below, scales would offer more protection than his human skin.

Arün crashed into the deep water of the bay. It felt like he was back inside the caldrun. Bubbles surrounded him as he kicked towards the surface. He needed to get to shore—there were creatures living in the waters of Arburaan that the forest predators feared even more than each other.

Arün's head broke the surface, and he scanned the waterline. Moonlight glinted off the dark ripples in the bay. To his right was the open ocean. A few hundred yards to his left, a beach stretched away from the towering cliffs. A massive doorway had been built into the cliff wall. Warm light spilled out onto the sand from inside the open entrance. The light glinted off hulking shapes spaced out in rows along the beach. Hundreds of elves moved between the giant forms.

What were they doing?

Arün swam forward, angling towards the darker part of the beach, further away from the cliff door. He needed to stay in the shadows, especially in his partially shifted form. The elves would be on alert and it was just a matter of time before the High Guard sent a search party to see whether he'd survived the fall.

The doorway had to be an entrance into the Vaults—a labyrinth of caverns and passageways that the elves had carved beneath the rocky peninsula. It was said that the Vaults guarded their most treasured possessions, so why were they open and what were these giant shapes on the beach?

Arün reached the shallows and forced his body to shift back to human. Rocks dotted the sand, providing cover. He scrambled to the first one and surveyed the giant forms. They were Marionettes, or Marions, as the Tyros back at the College liked to call them—giant war machines that the Mages had built to help the elves and pixies defeat the dragon clans. After the Ash War, the Marions had been decommissioned and placed in the Vaults. That had been over a hundred years ago. So, why had the elves brought them out of storage?

If he could get close enough to hear the elves, he might find out what was going on. Arün edged forward, moving between the shadows cast by the towering war machines. The Marions were odd, some looked like giant humanoid robots, others resembled monstrous mechanical insects. Each one a different design intended to be the best solution for fighting dragons. He stopped behind one of the large beach rocks and peaked around the corner.

Two elves were checking something on the leg of a bipedal Marion. Their lilting voices drifted across the moonlit sand.

"—said we need to finish this group by sunrise and move them into the *wellow*."

Arün wished he understood Elvish better —*wellow* could mean anything.

The second elf nodded. "Yes, we are to begin *bregana* tomorrow—"

Arün wasn't certain, but *bregana*—might be Elvish for *training*.

The first elf connected some wires. "I've never piloted one."

The other elf patted him on the shoulder. "You will learn. I was a pilot during the War."

The first elf's eyes went wide.

Arün frowned. Why were the elves training to pilot the Marionettes? The dracuns were no longer a threat. So why re-activate these war machines? And, if this new danger was so great, why hadn't the High Court notified the Mage Council?

He needed to keep moving. Whatever was going on, was secondary to locating Nadja.

One of the elves working on the Marion removed a dagger from his belt to cut a wire. As he drew the blade it flared bright orange. He shouted to the other elf who also drew his dagger.

Arün had seen these blades. They were similar to his Warden scryth, but more sensitive. They could detect the dracun part of him. Arün cursed as he ducked behind the rock. With his enhanced reflexes, he might be able to neutralize the elves—if he could take them by surprise.

He waited, but the elves didn't advance. Where had they gone?

Arün risked a glance around the rock.

One elf was running back toward the Vault entrance, but where was the other one?

The ground shook as the massive machine the elves had been working on rumbled to life. Bright lights mounted on the Marion chased away the shadows.

Arün pressed his back against the rock. He had to get off the beach, but if he ran, the Marion would rip him apart. Arün had seen what Marionettes could do. If the gatling guns in the arms weren't enough, it was bristling with other armaments that would reduce him to charcoal. There was only one chance to survive—and the opportunity wouldn't last long if any other Marions joined the hunt.

He vaulted the rock. The machine lowered its arms and sprayed bullets in his direction. Geysers of sand erupted from the ground around Arün. The elf piloting the Marion must be rusty—he wasn't leading his target.

Arün breathed a silent prayer of thanks as he reached the space between the machine's legs. It couldn't track him anymore. He had a choice now. Try to disable the Marion or use the pilot's confusion to escape? He decided to keep moving, disabling the Marion would waste valuable time.

While the machine was still facing the other direction, Arün continued his sprint towards the next Marion parked on the beach. The others were dormant and would serve as both cover and effective obstacles. Far away, a group of elves advanced from the Vault doorway. The elf in the lead was directing the others towards the Marions parked closest to the cliff entrance.

Arün angled away from the ocean as he weaved through the legs of the nearby machines.

The ground shook. The bipedal Marion had maneuvered around and was chasing him. Arün now regretted not choosing to disable it.

The Marion fired its guns.

Arün ducked behind the leg of one of the parked giants. Bullets ricocheted off the armored plating.

Two more Marion's rumbled to life closer to the Vault entrance. One looked like a giant spider—the other like some kind of mechanical dog. Either of them was more than capable of turning him into a bloody stain. Their lights turned on as they moved towards his position.

If Elek was here, he'd already have one of the Marion's activated and be getting them off the beach —but he wasn't.

More bullets ricocheted off the armor plating of the leg. Arün would be cornered soon. The only escape plan he could think of had dangerous polit- ical repercussions—he could shift into his dracun form and fly away.

More bullets pinged against the armor. The

Marion's were getting close. It wouldn't be long before they switched to other weapons. He had to leave now.

Arün stripped off his wet clothes and tied them into a bundle. He'd have to try to hold on to them while flying or he'd have nothing to wear when he shifted back. He placed the milkstone locket in his mouth. If he lost it, he'd never find Nadja.

Arün shifted into part-dracun form, grabbed his clothes and climbed to the top of the parked Marion using his green scaled claws to grip the riveted metal. The lights from the approaching machines filled the foggy air.

He dove off the shoulder of the Marionette. A spray of bullets filled the place where he'd just been standing. As he fell, Arün shifted into a full dracun. His emerald wings caught the air, and he angled toward the open water. Bullets chased his retreating form.

5

THE CAPITAL

ARÜN

Arün grunted as a bullet pierced his wing. He gritted his fangs at the stinging sensation and skimmed low over the dark bay. He hoped the maneuver would make it harder for the machines to target him. Many Marionette designs were capable of flight. Either he'd gotten lucky, and these models didn't have that functionality, or the pilots weren't skilled enough to risk chasing him over open water.

The beach disappeared into the fog and Arün breathed a sigh of relief. The cliffs rose to his right. Above them the walls and towers of the Capital shone in the darkness.

Arün beat his wings to gain altitude. Nadja was somewhere inside those walls.

The elves had built the city at the end of the

peninsula where the elevation was greatest. The ground sloped away from the Capital as the peninsula widened and blended into the mainland. From this elevation, Arün could see how the elves had terraced the land within the Capital walls to create five districts. Each district was a hundred feet higher than the next—forming natural walls within the outer wall. The city was a beautiful mix of graceful geometric forms intertwined with nature.

It did nothing to set him at ease.

Arün banked toward the tallest towers that housed the members of the High Court and searched for a place to land. He expected to see a volley of fire arrows, but the Capital was quiet. Why hadn't the High Guard sounded the alarm? Were the elves celebrating the holiday within an inner chamber?

Arün landed on the roof of one of the palace buildings and shifted back to his human form. As a dracun, he hadn't noticed the breeze coming off the bay, but now the wind sent a chill through his body. Flying around as a dracun was dangerous, but at least the elves couldn't corner him in the sky. He spit out the milkstone locket and snapped it open. The largest of the three dark spots on the stone pointed off to his right. He pulled on his pants and shifted to a form where he could use his wings while his body remained human.

Arün jumped off the rooftop and glided between the ivy coated spires while keeping an eye on the locket. It took two loops through the structures to decide that Nadja was somewhere inside the east tower. Arün angled toward a narrow bridge midway up the building that connected the tower to its neighbor. He landed on the empty span and shifted back into human form—back to normal. Arün pulled on the rest of his damp clothes.

The bridge led to a tall wooden door set into the tower. Arün moved forward—staying alert for any tightening in his chest that might warn him of a nearby ward. He looked out over the palace. Light spilled out of windows around the complex, but he saw no movement. No patrols. No sentries. No one from the High Court roaming the grounds.

It felt like a trap.

Arün reached the tower door and turned the latch. It swung inward onto a landing lit by a glowing crystal mounted on the curved wall. Green carpeted stairs spiraled upward to the left and downward to the right. There was a carved door on the opposite side of the landing. The interior had none of the gloom that Arün associated with castles on

Earth. The elvish architecture was simple and elegant. Under other circumstances, it would have been relaxing—but not now.

The locket showed that Nadja was somewhere farther below. Arün closed the door to the bridge and headed down the staircase. His footsteps made no sound on the thick carpeting as he descended. The spot on the milkstone grew larger as he spiraled down past landings, each with an identical carved door lit by a glowing crystal. At the base of the tower he emerged into an empty antechamber. Large doors led outside to the left, but the locket pointed right, toward a tall set of inner doors.

Arün crossed to them and pressed his ear against the wood.

Silence.

Where had everyone gone? The entire place felt abandoned. He opened the door a crack and slipped through the gap into a long moonlit hall. Large white pillars spaced at intervals held the high ceiling aloft. The columns were constructed to look like tree trunks—the carved branches interlaced overhead to form the ceiling. Moonlight spilled through glass panels set into the spaces between the limbs. Ivy climbed the supports and hung from the ceiling.

At the far end of the shadowy hall, atop a short flight of steps, sat a throne. Someone was sitting in it.

Arün checked the locket. It pointed across the expanse.

"Nadja?"

He didn't yell her name, but his voice echoed in the space as if he had.

The figure didn't move or answer.

Arün drew his gun and stepped deeper into the large room. The quiet was unsettling. He'd expected to find her held captive or squirreled away in a tiny room within the palace. Not here.

Along the sides of the hall, between each set of columns, was a pair of closed double doors. The High Guard could be hidden behind any of them— or all of them. At least the room was big enough to allow him to shift into a full dracun, and the ceiling appeared thin enough to break through if he needed to escape in a hurry. He hoped it wouldn't come to that.

Arün crept forward. "Nadja, is that you?"

Silence.

He descended a short flight of steps that mirrored the ones at the opposite side of the room and walked towards the center of the hall. His footsteps echoed off the walls.

The figure raised its head. "I knew you'd come."

It was Nadja.

A wave of relief swept over him, but now came the hard part. He had to ask for her forgiveness.

Arün scanned the side doors as he approached. "Are you okay?"

Nadja stood. She was wearing a green cloak. Her blond hair was tied back in the fashion of the elves. She held out her arm. In her hand, she grasped the chain of the milkstone locket linked to the one Arün held in his own hand. "I've been waiting for you."

"Nadja, I'm sorry. I tried to contact you—to explain—"

"I know," she interrupted.

Arün stopped at the foot of the steps. "I'm not what you think—I'm not a dracun. The Mages did this. We were trying to perfect a process to increase Warden survival rates. To make us better protectors."

Nadja's lips pressed together as she nodded. "I believe you and I understand why you hid it from me."

Arün swallowed a lump that was forming in his throat. He didn't realize how much he had needed to hear those words. "You're not angry?" His voice came out as a whisper.

"Not at you, Arün. You helped me see clearly for

the first time—to understand what needs to be done."

"What do you mean?"

Nadja lowered her hand. "The dragon clans should have never been exiled to Earth. They should have been eradicated. Now the Mages are trying to integrate them into our society—mix them into the human gene pool. I don't blame you, Arün—you thought you were helping. But, those creatures don't belong in our world. We'll fix that mistake."

"What are you—"

Arün felt the pin-prick of pain near his throat at the same instant he realized that they weren't alone. He reached up and plucked the dart from his neck.

His vision blurred. He'd ignored his instincts and walked into the trap.

"Nadja—"

He collapsed to the floor before he could finish the thought.

"Wake him." The voice was deep and melodic.

Cold water splashed against Arün's face.

He opened his eyes to find he was strapped to a metal chair. Water dripped down his back, soaking his shirt. There was something around his neck with sharp points that pressed against his throat.

His eyes struggled to gain focus. He was in a small windowless room lit by a single glowing crystal. An elf in an intricate embroidered gray robe stood across from him.

Nadja entered Arün's view as she stepped around from behind the chair, a dripping bucket held in her hand. She leaned forward and wiped the water from his face with a soft towel. "I'm sorry, Arün. The King didn't want to take any chances."

The elf in the robes stepped forward. "I am Athren, king of this realm." He held Arün's scryth. "And you are a Warden, but your actions speak otherwise."

Arün didn't answer. They'd knocked him out and bound him. They could have killed him, but they hadn't. So, what did they want? Was he alive because of Nadja or because they needed something from him?

The King pointed the scryth at Arün. "You're wearing a collar embedded with blades like this scryth. If you try to change form, they will pierce your neck and react with your blood most unpleasantly."

Arün forced a smile onto his face. "I bet you're Santa's favorite elf."

The King's eyes narrowed. "What do you mean?"

Nadja dropped the bucket. "He means nothing."

Arün locked eyes with her. "You lured me here. What do you want?" He wished he could speak into her mind. There were things he needed to say, but not in front of the elf.

"It was the only way, Arün."

He glared at his partner. She had manipulated him.

The King's voice boomed. "You will teach us the weave to open the Thorngate or you will die for violating our laws."

Arün's jaw dropped. This was why they'd let him live—they wanted to use one of the Thorngates to cross over to Earth. The Mages guarded and controlled access to the gates. The weave to activate the growth of the tunnel was a secret—they had only taught it to Arün so he could complete the mission to rescue Alley.

"Even if I showed it to you—I don't know the rune sequence required to open the portal," he growled at the elf. It was a two-stage process. Step on a sequence of runes to open the portal, then cast the weave to grow the vine tunnel required for safe passage across the space between the two worlds.

Nadja withdrew a map from under her cloak. "We have the rune sequence."

Arün recognized the parchment. It was the map they'd used on their last mission that had an inscription of the correct rune order. Nadja had held onto it so that the knowledge to open the gate would be kept separate from the weave to grow the tunnel.

Arün stared at the floor. What were they planning? Why would they go to Earth without the Council's permission? His eyes went wide.

They had opened the Vaults.

They were re-activating the Marionettes on the beach.

They were preparing for an invasion.

Arün looked up at his partner. "What have you done, Nadja?"

"I found allies who share my conviction—"

Athren nodded. "That we need a permanent end to the dragon threat."

Arün glared at the King. "The Council and the Clans won't let you—"

Nadja interrupted him with a laugh. "They won't know we're coming."

The King clasped his hands. "You must choose

now, Warden. Help us and live or oppose us and face judgment."

Nadja touched Arün's cheek. "When this over we won't have to be Wardens anymore. We can live normal lives again. Our world and this one, will be safe—forever."

Arün hung his head.

He didn't want to die.

He didn't want to help start a war.

Brody had been right. This mission was a terrible idea.

THE END

The adventure will continue in
Emerald City Dragons - Book 2!

AUTHOR'S NOTE

Thank you for taking a chance on a new author—for coming on an adventure with me. Without you, there would be no story—just text on a page. It's your imagination, your emotions, your experiences that breath unique life into these words.

If you enjoyed reading the *The Lost Warden*, I would be grateful if you could take a few moments to leave a brief review on the book's Amazon page. Reviews help increase the visibility of my books on the store so that other people like yourself can discover and enjoy them!

Visit: **wesleygrandmont.com/books** and click on the Amazon link for *The Lost Warden* to leave a review.

While you're visiting my site, if you're not already a member of my Reader Group, you can join by clicking the button on the main page. I'll send you my monthly newsletter which includes behind-the-scenes information on new and upcoming releases, as well as lots of other great surprises!

Thank you so much for being one of my readers!

-Wes Grandmont III

ABOUT THE AUTHOR

Wesley Grandmont III is a writer, artist and game developer who is passionate about crafting immersive worlds for his readers. He writes stories that mix the modern world with magic—urban fantasies with the tension and pacing of espionage thrillers. His debut book series *Emerald City Dragons*, is an urban fantasy world set in and around Seattle.

A seasoned veteran of the video game industry, Wes has worked on over twenty games, most recently as Lead Technical Art Director on Microsoft's *Halo 5 : Guardians*, and Sony's *Ghost of Tsushima*.

When not crafting new stories or games, he loves coffee (lots of coffee), skiing, hiking and spending time with family and friends in the Pacific Northwest.

 facebook.com/WesGrandmontAuthor

ALSO BY WES GRANDMONT III

Make sure to check out all the books in the *Emerald City Dragons* series!

The Alley of Secrets

The Obsidian Ascent

The Lost Warden